PUFFIN BOOKS

Smasher

Dick King-Smith served in the Grenadier Guards during the Second World War, and afterwards spent twenty years as a farmer in Gloucestershire, the county of his birth. Many of his stories are inspired by his farming experiences. Later he taught at a village primary school. His first book, *The Fox Busters*, was published in 1978. Since then he has written a great number of children's books, including *The Sheep-Pig* (winner of the *Guardian* Award and filmed as *Babe*), *Harry's Mad*, *Noah's Brother*, *The Hodgeheg*, *Martin's Mice*, *Ace*, *The Cuckoo Child* and *Harriet's Hare* (winner of the Children's Book Award in 1995). At the British Book Awards in 1992 he was voted Children's Author of the Year. He is married, with three children and eleven grandchildren, and lives in a seventeenth-century cottage a short crow's-flight from the house where he was born.

DICK KING-SMITH
Smasher

Illustrated by Mike Terry

PUFFIN BOOKS

PUFFIN BOOKS

Published by the Penguin Group
Penguin Books Ltd, 27 Wrights Lane, London W8 5TZ, England
Penguin Putnam Inc., 375 Hudson Street, New York, New York 10014, USA
Penguin Books Australia Ltd, Ringwood, Victoria, Australia
Penguin Books Canada Ltd, 10 Alcorn Avenue, Toronto, Ontario, Canada M4V 3B2
Penguin Books (NZ) Ltd, 182–190 Wairau Road, Auckland 10, New Zealand

Penguin Books Ltd, Registered Offices: Harmondsworth, Middlesex, England

First published by Viking 1996
Published in Puffin Books 1998
10

Text copyright © Fox Busters Ltd, 1996
Illustrations copyright © Mike Terry, 1996
All rights reserved

The moral right of the author and illustrator has been asserted

Filmset in Palatino

Made and printed in England by Clays Ltd, St Ives plc

British Library Cataloguing in Publication Data
A CIP catalogue record for this book is available from the British Library

ISBN 0–140–37797–2

Contents

1. The Ugly Puppy

"Kindest thing I could do for you," said Farmer Buzzard, "would be to knock you on the head."

He stood in the stable looking down into a shallow wooden box filled with straw, where his collie bitch Kay lay nursing her litter of newborn puppies.

He was not talking to Kay, though she wagged at the sound of his voice.

He was not talking to three of the four puppies, who were all black-and-white miniatures of their mother.

He was talking to the fourth puppy.

The fourth puppy looked nothing like the others. It was bigger, it was the colour of milky coffee, and it had a very large blunt head with a wrinkled face. It looked, in short, like a freak.

Farmer Buzzard bent down and picked up the fourth puppy in one large hand and held it in front of his face.

"Good job your eyes is closed, my son," he said to it, "because if you was to catch sight of yourself in a mirror, you'd have a fit, you would. I never seed anything so ugly in all my born days. You're not going to be no use to no one. I got to do away with you. I'll be doing you a favour."

As though she could understand his words, Kay whined softly.

"All right, all right," said Farmer Buzzard. "Keep un for now, old girl." And he put the fourth puppy back with the rest and walked out of the stable.

In the kitchen of the farmhouse, Mrs Buzzard had breakfast ready. As some married couples do, the Buzzards looked strangely alike, so that they might have been taken for brother and sister. Both were tall and angular with strong curved noses, and strangers sometimes thought them well named, so much did they put them in mind of a pair of big birds of prey. Oddly, Mrs Buzzard had been a Miss Hawk before she got married.

Now she said, as she had said every mealtime for the past thirty years, "Wash your hands."

Farmer Buzzard washed them. As he

stood drying them, he said, "Kay's whelped."

"How many pups?" asked Mrs Buzzard.

"Four."

"All right, are they?"

"Three are. Look just like Kay."

"What's up with t'other?"

"Martha," said Farmer Buzzard solemnly, "he's the ugliest puppy you ever did see. Who the father of them is I do not know, but to see this puppy you'd think his dad was the Hound of the Baskervilles. I shall have to knock him on the head."

Mrs Buzzard smiled. She knew how tender-hearted her husband was, and she put a plate of bacon and eggs in front of him and said, "Eat your breakfast, Ken, and then you can go and put the poor little creature out of his misery. A little runt, is he?"

"No," said Farmer Buzzard. "He's the biggest."

"Weakly, then?"

"No, the strongest."

"Just ugly?"

"Aye," said Farmer Buzzard. "Ugly as sin."

"Dear, dear," said Mrs Buzzard.

At the end of the morning when her husband came in for his midday meal, she said, "Done it then?"

"Done what?" said Farmer Buzzard.

"Put that puppy down."

"Oh no, I forgot. Been that busy."

In the afternoon Mrs Buzzard went out with a bucket of corn and a basket, to feed her hens and collect their eggs. On her way back she went into the stable to see Kay and her litter. The three black-and-white puppies were all asleep, full fed, but the big brown puppy was still nursing busily, and the look of pride on the collie bitch's face told Mrs Buzzard just what the mother thought of this hideous child.

"Don't you fret, my girl," she said to the dog. "He won't never harm un. He's too soft."

That evening after tea she said to her husband, "Treat yourself to a glass of beer, I should. 'Twill make you feel better. It must have been a hard thing to do."

"Feel better?" said Farmer Buzzard.

"Hard thing? What are you on about?"

"Killing that puppy, of course."

Farmer Buzzard grinned sheepishly.

"I never," he said.

"Why ever not?"

"Not his fault he looks like he does. You never know, he might get better-looking when he's growed."

"Can't fail to," said Mrs Buzzard.

"You know what, Martha?" said her
husband. "I think I'll have that glass of
beer. You like anything?"

"I shouldn't mind a drop of port," said
Mrs Buzzard, and when her husband had
fetched the glasses, she said, "We'll drink
his health, shall us?"

"What, that puppy?"

"Yes. And he ought to have a name,
now that you've decided to keep him."

"Don't know about keeping him," said Farmer Buzzard. "I shall be selling all the puppies once they're old enough."

"Reckon anyone will want him? Seeing he's so ugly? Perhaps that's what we'd better call him. 'Ugly.' After all, even if he does improve in looks, he's never going to be a smasher, is he?"

"'Smasher'!" said Farmer Buzzard. "That's it! That's what we'll call him!" and they touched glasses and drank.

2. Chicken Chasing

Eight weeks later, Farmer Buzzard put an advertisement in the local paper, which read:

COLLIE PUPPIES FOR SALE, TWO DOGS,
ONE BITCH, FROM GOOD WORKING MOTHER
STEADY ON SHEEP OR CATTLE.

When Mrs Buzzard read it, she said, "I see you've only advertised three."

"That's right," said her husband.

"Well, well," said Mrs Buzzard.

Over the next few days several people came to look at the puppies.

The first was another farmer, a neighbour of the Buzzards, and he knew exactly what he wanted.

"I'll have the bitch puppy, Ken," he said. "I've always fancied having a daughter of your Kay's, she's a good un, she is."

He squatted on his heels and patted the three black-and-white pups.

"Nice level lot," he said. "Who's the father?"

"Oh, you wouldn't know him," said Farmer Buzzard.

At that moment Smasher, who had been playing by himself in a far corner of the stable, came bumbling up, pushing his rather smaller brothers and sister out of his way, and licked the neighbour's hand with a large slobbery tongue.

"What's this then?" said the neighbour. "He's never out of the same litter, is he?"

Farmer Buzzard nodded.

"Throwback," he said.

"Throwback!" said the neighbour. "I reckon I'd have thrown him out."

He looked at the brown puppy, noting

the size of his feet and the folds of loose
skin on his big face.

"He's more like a bull mastiff than a
collie, he is," he said. "Puts me in mind of
that guard dog that Fred Selman used to
have, up at Hollybush Farm. What an
object! However did your Kay come to
have one like that?"

"Dunno," said Farmer Buzzard.

"Ain't he ever ugly!" said the

neighbour, and when there was no reply to this, added, "Well, he's no beauty, Ken, is he?"

"Not pertickerly," said Farmer Buzzard.

"You going to keep him?"

"Dunno. I might."

The second man to come in search of a puppy was obviously short-sighted. He wore a pair of thick spectacles, and when he was shown the three remaining puppies, pointed straight at Smasher and said, "I'll have the brown one."

For a split second Farmer Buzzard was tempted. Here was the one chance of a home for the ugly puppy (which he didn't need to keep – Kay did all the work of the farm with no trouble). Nobody but the half-blind man would have picked him.

The farmer looked at Smasher's large wrinkled face, turned up to him with a sort of grin on it.

"Sorry," he said, "the brown un's not for sale. There's two other dog puppies to pick from."

"You choose one of them for me then," said the short-sighted man. "My sight's not so good these days. Pity about the

brown one though. A fine-looking little chap, from what I can see."

That same day the other black-and-white dog puppy was sold to another farmer, and Smasher was left alone with his mother.

That night as he lay beside her in the stable, he said, thoughtfully, "I don't look much like you, Mum, do I?"

Kay surveyed her remaining child. Poor little chap, she thought.

"No, dear," she said. "Not a lot."

"And I don't look like my brothers or my sister did."

"No, dear. You must take after your father."

"What was he like, Mum?"

"Tall. And dark."

"And handsome?"

"Oh yes," said Kay.

"So when I grow up, I'll be tall, dark

and handsome, shall I, Mum?"

"Of course you will, dear," said Kay.
"Of course you will."

That night as she lay in bed beside her
husband, Mrs Buzzard said, thoughtfully,
"What are you going to do with him then,
Ken?"

"Who?" said Farmer Buzzard sleepily.

"Smasher. Going to train him to work
sheep?"

"No. He got no gift for that," said
Farmer Buzzard, for he had noticed that,
while the other three puppies had begun
to try to herd his wife's chickens about
the farmyard, Smasher had taken no part
in this instinctive sheepdog behaviour.
His only occasional contribution had been
to rush at a hen, open-mouthed, and try
to grab hold of it. The farmer had not told
his wife this.

"Well, what have you kept him for then?" asked Mrs Buzzard. "Not for his looks surely? Come on, admit it, you've just got a soft spot for him, haven't you?"

"Not pertickerly," said Farmer Buzzard. But he had.

It was just as well that he had, because, some weeks later, Smasher went looking for trouble. Not only was he growing fast, he was also faster on his feet, and he started to chase chickens in earnest.

Feathers began to fly, and, fearing that blood would soon be spilled, Kay gave her son a good talking-to.

"Smasher," she said (for, hearing his name on the farmer's lips, she had learned it, just as, long ago, she had learned her own), "you are *not* to chase chickens. Do you understand?"

"Why not, Mum?"

"Because if my master catches you doing it, he will beat you."

"Why, Mum?"

"Because dogs are not allowed to chase chickens."

"Why not, Mum?"

"Because people don't like that."

"Why, Mum?"

Kay lost patience.

"Oh be quiet!" she growled. "And don't

you dare say, 'Why, Mum?'" and she
walked away.

"Why not, Mum?" said Smasher under
his breath. Chicken chasing is fun, he
thought, and next day he waited until his
mother had left the yard with the farmer
to go round the sheep, and then he went
into action.

Mrs Buzzard was making bread, when she heard through the open kitchen window a frantic chorus of shrieks and squawks, and, looking out, saw hens flapping madly everywhere as the big brown puppy galloped clumsily among them. Some birds in their panic fluttered into the duckpond, and after them rushed Smasher, and after him ran Mrs Buzzard on her long thin legs, a rolling-pin in her floury hand and a string of angry words on her lips.

Smasher fled and the waterlogged hens floundered to safety and Mrs Buzzard fumed. She had quite a temper and she was very angry.

"What d'you think your dog's been up to?" said Mrs Buzzard when she next saw her husband.

"My dog?" said Farmer Buzzard. "She's been with me, all morning."

"No, not Kay. Your puppy, that Smasher. Only chasing my chickens, that's all. Drove some of them into the duckpond and half drowned them."

"Oh," said Farmer Buzzard.

"No good you standing there saying 'Oh'," said Mrs Buzzard. "He wants a beating, he does, teach him a lesson."

Farmer Buzzard went to find Smasher. No good beating him now, he thought, he

won't understand what it's for. Have to catch him in the act.

Smasher was lying beside his mother in the stable with his ugly head on his paws, looking as though butter wouldn't melt in his big mouth.

"He's been a bad boy, Kay," said Farmer Buzzard softly. "You ought to have learned him better."

Then he picked up a length of rope, and

with it he struck six hard blows on an old canvas tarpaulin that was hung from the roof beam to dry.

"Naughty dog!" shouted Farmer Buzzard loudly as he whacked the tarpaulin, while Kay and Smasher looked on in astonishment.

"Sounds like you gave him what for," said Mrs Buzzard when her husband returned. "Didn't hit him too hard, I hope? He's only little." She was already regretting making the farmer punish Smasher.

"No," said Farmer Buzzard.

"He's a brave one though," said his wife. "I could hear you beating him plain as plain, yet he never made a sound."

"No," said Farmer Buzzard.

"The master sounded angry," said Smasher to his mother when Farmer Buzzard had gone.

"Yes," said Kay, thoughtfully.

She looked carefully at her son. Stuck to the corner of his mouth, she could see, was a single small wet white feather.

"You've been chasing those chickens again," she said.

"Just for fun, Mum," said Smasher. "I won't do it again," he said.

Or not while you're around, he thought.

"You better not," Kay said.

Because, she thought, puppies that chase chickens could well end up as dogs that chase sheep. And dogs that chase sheep could well end up dead.

3. As Good as Gold

Up till now, Smasher had not been allowed into the farmhouse. Once or twice he had tried to follow Kay in, but Mrs Buzzard had always shooed him out again.

"You stop out in the stable, my lad," she had said. "You can make as much mess as you like out there."

But then she changed her mind, for two reasons. One was on account of her hens. He needs watching, that puppy does, she thought, while Ken and Kay are out round the farm. That's when he gets into mischief. Better if he's with me, then I can keep my eye on him.

The second reason was that she felt guilty. I never should have told Ken to beat him, she said to herself (and that

hard too, it's not like him). After all, he's only a puppy even though he's growed so big, as big as his mother he is already.

So one morning, when the farmer and the collie bitch had gone out on their rounds, Mrs Buzzard opened the back door and called, "Smasher!"

She called, had she known it, in the nick of time, for Smasher was just about to have a go at one of her hens, which had most unwisely wandered into the stable.

Smasher was lying quite still, pretending to be asleep. I'll corner this one, he thought, I know Mum said I shouldn't but this is too good a chance to miss.

Then he heard his name called.

What a great thing he's getting, thought Mrs Buzzard as she watched him lumbering across the yard towards her. He's not got any better looking but maybe he's got more sensible. He hasn't bothered the hens lately. She reeled as, unable to stop in time, he bumped into her legs.

"Steady!" she said. "Clumsy great elephant," and she turned back into the house.

Smasher sat down outside the open back door. He did not expect to be invited in. He had discussed this with his mother.

"Why don't they want me in the house, Mum?" he had said.

"Because you're a yard dog," said Kay. "Not a house dog."

"But you go in, and you're a sheepdog, not a house dog."

"I'm both, dear," said Kay. "I know how to behave properly indoors."

So now it was with surprise that he heard Mrs Buzzard calling, "Smasher. Come along in. Good boy."

Ears cocked, he hurried through the door and along a passage that led to the kitchen. The passageway was dark, and Smasher did not see that at one side of it there was a tall old-fashioned umbrella-stand holding a clutch of walking-sticks and hung with many mackintoshes and coats and hats – until he barged straight into it.

It fell down with a great clatter, and the mass of clothing buried him.

"Clumsy as a *herd* of elephants, I should have said!" cried Mrs Buzzard as she put everything in order again.

While she was doing this, she heard a loud racket in the kitchen. Smasher had upset a large tin basin full of dog's drinking-water which now streamed across the floor.

"What next!" cried Mrs Buzzard. Her question was soon answered.

As ill luck would have it, Mrs Buzzard was preparing to make jam that day, and had put ready, on a low wooden bench close to the stove, a double rank of glass screwtop jars.

As she knelt on the kitchen floor, mopping up the water, Smasher, seeing her for the first time down at his own

level on hands and knees, thought she was playing some sort of game. Eagerly he bounded forward to lick her face, his long thick tail whipping madly from side to side. Each stroke of it sent jam-jars tumbling off the bench to smash to pieces on the flagged floor.

How aptly was he named at that moment.

"Smasher!" screamed Mrs Buzzard. "You bad dog, you!" And she stood up and grabbed a mop. She aimed a furious blow at the puppy, a blow which broke the remaining jam-jars, while Mrs Buzzard slipped on the wet floor and fell flat on her back.

When she got to her feet once more, Smasher was nowhere to be seen.

"Only meself to blame," grumbled Mrs Buzzard as she went down the passage to shut the back door.

"And you can stop out!" she shouted down the yard as she closed it. "Should have had more sense than to let you in in the first place!"

Smasher, however, was still in the house.

Bewildered by the crash of breaking glass and the sound of Mrs Buzzard's angry voice and the fact that she was trying to hit him, he had bolted out of the kitchen through the nearest door, into another of the many passageways that threaded the rambling old farm-house. A little way along it was a small room from which a most attractive smell came to Smasher's blunt nose.

Curious, he looked into the larder and saw, upon a marble slab, a large piece of meat. Carefully, for he could still hear Mrs Buzzard's angry voice in the distance, he took the leg of lamb in his mouth, and proceeded down the passage till he came to another room.

This was Mrs Buzzard's front parlour, a room which was her pride and joy, never used except when there was special company. It contained two large armchairs and a sofa, all upholstered in a kind of pale blue velvet, and a number of small slender-legged tables on which stood a great many china ornaments.

Something told Smasher he had better lie low for a bit.

Earlier that morning he had been down to the duckpond for a drink and a little paddle. His large feet (though Mrs Buzzard had not noticed this) had on their pads a good deal of mud, mostly composed of duck muck. It had dried, but now the water spilled on the kitchen floor had wetted it again.

Smasher padded across the room, carrying the leg of lamb, and the carpet, which was a cream colour, acquired a brand-new pattern.

He hoisted himself up on to the sofa and tucked in to the meat.

This is more comfortable than the stable, he thought, when only the bone was left. I'll have a nap now.

After a while Smasher woke suddenly. He felt an urgent need. He had drunk a great deal of water from the duckpond, and now he needed to get rid of some of it.

Only a few days ago he had, for the first time ever, not squatted as puppies do but cocked his leg against the stable doorpost.

"Watch me, Mum," he had said. "You can't do that, can you?"

"I don't do that," said Kay.

Now he cocked his leg against the side of the blue velvet sofa and then, for luck, against each of the armchairs.

Handy trick that is, he said to himself with a sigh of relief, better than squatting in the middle of the carpet. She might not

have liked that. Now then, if I'm going to be a house dog, I'd better have a good look round the place.

He wandered out of the parlour and along the passage till he came to the foot of a flight of stairs. Smasher humped himself up these and saw, facing the head of the stairs, an open bedroom door.

It was the Buzzards' bedroom, and on the Buzzards' bed, as yet unmade, was a candlewick bedspread, fringed with rows of little round bobbles. After trying unsuccessfully to jump up on the bed, Smasher contented himself with chewing off a great many of the bobbles.

Then he turned his attention to the bottom of the curtains and altered their shape a good deal. Then he found Mrs Buzzard's mules and chewed up the left one. Then he came across Farmer Buzzard's bedroom slippers and chewed up one of those (the right one, as it happened).

After that, bored with chewing things, Smasher decided to go downstairs again. They were quite steep, and he fell most of the way.

Passing the parlour door once more, he looked in. There, on the sofa, sniffing at the lamb-bone, *his* lamb bone, was one of Mrs Buzzard's cats.

Furiously, Smasher rushed at it, overturning a couple of little tables on his way into the room and another couple on his way out after the fleeing cat, while china ornaments flew everywhere.

The cat dashed out through the back door, which Mrs Buzzard had left open while she went down the yard to make sure that Smasher wasn't after her hens.

Smasher followed, but the cat was much

too quick for him and he gave up the chase.

Smasher made his way to the stable and lay down, full of lamb and tired out by his morning's work.

A few minutes later Mrs Buzzard looked in and saw him lying there.

"Bless him," she said as she made her way back to the farmhouse.

"There's me thinking the worst of him and all the time he's lying there as good as gold."

In the kitchen she looked up at the clock on the wall, and said, "Now then, I must make the bed and dust the front parlour and then I'll put that nice leg of lamb on to cook . . ."

4. The Field-barn

"And on top of all that," said Mrs Buzzard, "he wetted on my three-piece suite!"

She had just finished detailing to her husband the damage done by the puppy, his puppy. She was absolutely furious.

"Add it all together," she said, "and you're looking at a hundred pounds worth and more. You named him well, you did."

"Oh," said Farmer Buzzard.

"No good you standing there saying 'Oh'," replied Mrs Buzzard. "What are you going to do about it, that's what I'm asking?"

"Dunno."

"Well, I do. That animal is never coming inside my house again, never. Which I

dare say he'll try to do unless I keeps every door shut from now on. Which I'm not prepared to do, this fine weather. So there's only one answer."

"What's that, Martha?" said Farmer Buzzard.

"You got to get rid of him."

"Sell him, you mean?"

"Don't know about sell him," said Mrs Buzzard. "Nobody would buy such an ugly creature, not unless 'twas a half-blind man."

"You surely don't mean," said Farmer Buzzard, "that you want me to . . ." He stopped, unable to complete the sentence.

"I don't care what you does, Ken," said Mrs Buzzard, her eyes flashing, "just so long as he's gone. After today, I never wants to set eyes on him again."

Meanwhile, in the stable, Smasher was saying, "Guess what, Mum."

"What, dear?"

"I think I'm going to be a house dog. I was invited in to the house today."

"Did you enjoy it?"

"Oh yes!" said Smasher. "It was smashing."

"I hope you behaved yourself," said Kay.

At that moment they saw the farmer

coming across the yard towards them. He
carried his gun in the crook of his arm.

He picked up the length of rope with
which he had once whacked the
tarpaulin, and tied it round Smasher's
neck. Then he set off with the two dogs,
Smasher cavorting excitedly on the end of

the rope, Kay trotting soberly at heel. Out through the yard gate they went and off across the fields.

Some time afterwards Mrs Buzzard, sitting at her sewing-machine repairing her tattered bedroom curtains, heard the bang of a distant gun.

"Oh, no!" she said. "He's surely never been and gone and . . ." she stopped, unable to complete the sentence.

"I heard a shot," she said when her husband returned.

"Rabbit," said Farmer Buzzard. "Missed him."

That evening Mrs Buzzard had no cause to go into the stable, but if she had, she would have found Kay there alone.

So busy was Mrs Buzzard with curtain mending, and bedspread mending, and the cleaning of carpet and furniture, and the repair of broken ornaments, and the collecting of replacement jam-jars that it was not until twenty-four hours later that she found time to say, "That Smasher. What have you done with him?"

"Found him a good home," said Farmer Buzzard.

"That's quick, then," said Mrs Buzzard with relief. "Difficult, was it, to place him?"

"Not pertickerly," said Farmer Buzzard.

At the far end of the farm there stood, in the middle of a field, an old stone barn with a walled yard in front of it. Here, in winter, Farmer Buzzard kept a dozen or so store cattle.

Now it contained one animal only – Smasher.

This was where the farmer had gone the previous day, gun in hand, one dog at heel, the other on a rope, while slung

across his back was his gamebag. In it was
a feeding-dish and a supply of dog food.

When they reached the field-barn,
Farmer Buzzard shut the gate of the yard
behind them and let Smasher off the rope.

He checked that there were some straw
bales inside the building, that the cattle-
trough was low enough for Smasher to
drink from and that the bars of the gate

were too close together for him to squeeze
between. The walls were too high to be
jumped.

It was a prison certainly, but a roomy
and comfortable one nevertheless, and a
perfect hiding-place. No one ever came
there but the farmer. Mrs Buzzard
certainly wouldn't. No one would know.

Farmer Buzzard sat down on a bale of

straw, and Smasher bumbled up and shoved his wrinkled face into his master's lap.

Farmer Buzzard did his best to explain the position to the exile.

"Now you listen here, my boy," he said, "while I puts you in the picture. You've blotted your copybook proper, you have, and my missus wants to see the back of you for good and all. She'd like me to take you to the Dogs' Home, I dare say. Or worse. Which I'm not going to do. And why not? Because I've growed fond of you, ugly and clumsy and destructive as you are. There's good in you somewheres, I'm sure of it. So you've got to stop here whether you likes it or not, and your mum and me, we'll come and visit you every day, to exercise you and to feed you, while we give things time to settle down at home."

"What was all that about, Mum?" asked Smasher as the farmer stood up and, cutting the strings of the straw bale he'd been sitting on, began to strew it about to make a bed.

Kay had not of course understood Farmer Buzzard's actual words, but she knew instinctively what was going to happen. Smasher, for some reason, was going to be kept down here in the

field-barn for the time being. He must have done something wrong. He's in the dog-house, she thought to herself.

"I think, dear," she said, "that the master was telling you that now you're a big boy – not a puppy any more but a dog – he's giving you your very own place to live. See, he's brought your feeding-dish and he's going to give you your supper now and a lovely supper it looks."

Farmer Buzzard put the loaded feeding-dish down on the floor, and Smasher tucked in.

Quietly the farmer said, "Come, Kay," and quickly they slipped out of the barn, through the yard, and out of the gate, which Farmer Buzzard latched behind them.

It's only for a few days, he said to himself as they walked home. Till the storm blows over.

But all the same he was worried at the thought of the dog left all alone, so much so that when a rabbit popped up right in front of them, he completely missed his shot.

When Smasher had finished his food, he went to the gate, through which, his nose told him, his mother and the master had gone. But it was closed. He tried to

squeeze between the bars, but he was too big.

Oh well, he thought, they'll be back in a minute. He was quite used to being on his own during the daytime, in the stable. He had a drink at the cattle-trough, went into the barn, lay down on his straw bed, and went to sleep.

When he woke again it was getting dark, and still they hadn't come back. Mum's always back by dark, he thought. Never in his short life had Smasher slept a night on his own.

He went to the gate again and looked out, but there was nothing to be seen except the distant lights of the farmhouse.

That's where I should be if I'm going to be a house dog, thought Smasher, not stuck out here, and he pointed his blunt snout at the sky and let out a long doleful howl.

In the stable Kay heard it. Poor boy, she thought, he's lonely.

In the house Mrs Buzzard heard it.

"What's that?" she said.

"Dog howling somewhere," said Farmer Buzzard.

"Not Kay, is it?"

"No, she's in the stable."

"Well, it can't be that Smasher," said Mrs Buzzard. "He's in his new home, I'm thankful to say. He'll soon settle down there."

"I hopes," said Farmer Buzzard.

5. A Stifled Sneeze

"Only a few days," Farmer Buzzard had said to himself, but two months later, Smasher was still living in the field-barn.

The more he thought about it, the more the farmer was sure that there was no point in bringing the dog back to the farm yet, much less in hoping that Smasher would be allowed in the house again. Mrs Buzzard was still so cross she would never allow it.

The return from exile could only possibly happen when Smasher was a fully trained animal.

"So," said Farmer Buzzard to Kay, "we must set about training this son of yours. He must have some of your brains, whoever his father was. And he's anxious to please, which is half the battle."

On this last point he was right. Smasher was indeed keen to be in the farmer's good books, and when, after that first evening, his mother told him that howling at night (or at any other time) was not a good idea, he did not howl again.

At first he thought of the field-barn as a prison with its own exercise yard, but as time went on, and Kay kept telling him how lucky he was to have such a place all to himself, Smasher began first to accept and then quite to enjoy his solitary life.

Nor was it all that solitary, for the master came with Kay three times every day. They came in the morning, on their rounds of the sheep and cattle, and again in the evening, when Smasher was fed. And in the middle of each day, in the early afternoon, Farmer Buzzard set aside a couple of hours for a training session.

He was by nature a good trainer of dogs, knowledgeable and firm and above all patient, and he was determined that this ugly dog of his should become a model pupil. Tearing things up in the house and making messes was puppy stuff, never to be repeated.

To put his teeth to proper use, he gave Smasher big marrow bones to gnaw, but the teaching of cleanliness was a more difficult problem.

The only way open to him, Farmer
Buzzard decided, was to pretend that the
field-barn was a house and teach Smasher
to do everything he had to do in the yard
outside. Barn-trained equalled house-
trained, he reckoned.

It took time, because Smasher couldn't
see the point of it, but Kay encouraged
him and the farmer rewarded him, and
soon it became habit.

In the meantime Smasher was taken

around the farm (always out of sight of
the house) on a leash, and taught to walk
at heel, and then (off the leash) to sit, and
at the command "Down!" to lie down,
and at "Stay!" to remain lying down, even
though the master should move away
from him. At first Farmer Buzzard only
took a few steps away, but before too long
he could walk half across a field and stop
and look back to see Smasher still lying
where he had been put. After the earlier
business with the chickens, Farmer
Buzzard was concerned that Smasher
might chase the cattle, or worse, the
sheep. But he need not have worried.
Smasher showed no interest in either.

The credit for this was Kay's.

The very first time that Smasher had
gone among the flock of sheep while off
the leash, he had made a little rush at a
lamb while the farmer's back was turned.

Farmer Buzzard looked round at the sound of a sudden growl followed by a sharp yelp of pain, to see Smasher holding up a paw and looking very sorry for himself. Kay, he saw, had her hackles up.

Perhaps he trod on her, he thought, he's clumsy enough and a lot bigger than her too.

"What's up, Kay?" he said, but she could not of course answer.

"Ow!" cried Smasher. "That hurt, Mum! What did you want to do that for?"

"To teach you a lesson, I hope," said Kay angrily. "I told you before what happens to dogs who chase sheep. I never want to see you chasing an animal on this farm again, ever, whether it's chickens or bullocks or sheep, do you understand?"

"Yes, Mum," said Smasher, licking his bitten paw.

"You're doing very well in your training," said Kay, "so don't go messing it up now. Say to yourself, whatever happens, I must always act sensibly."

"Yes, Mum," said Smasher. "If I do," he said, "d'you think I'll be a house dog in the end?"

"I don't know," said Kay.

She looked up at the farmer and whined a little, which meant, "D'you think he will be?" but he could not of course answer.

When two months had gone by, a major problem arose.

The time was fast approaching when Farmer Buzzard would need the field-barn and yard to house a dozen bullocks through the winter months. Then there would be no way that Smasher could stay. He might be barn-trained but the bullocks certainly weren't.

"I got no choice," said the farmer to Kay. "He'll have to come back up the farm. Can't take him in the house, Martha won't have it, but she might just put up with him being in the stable again. After all, time's passed since he did all that damage, and what's more, he's well-trained now."

Farmer Buzzard left things as late as he could, but it had been a wet autumn, and already the heavy bullocks were beginning to poach the fields, to tread the

grass, especially around the gateways and water-troughs, into a muddy mess.

"Anyways," he said to Kay, "with the cold weather coming we can't leave Smasher down here all through the winter. He needs to come in by the fire night times, like you do."

So he decided that the following Saturday he would yard the bullocks and bring Smasher back to the farm.

He did not try to prepare the way for this by any mention of his plan to his wife. She, after all, believed that the dog had been living with a new master for almost three months now.

"We'll just have to take a chance," he said to Smasher. "One thing's certain. I'm not getting rid of you." And he patted his ugly brown dog.

As he did so, it struck him how much Smasher had grown, what a big strong

animal he now was, and he remembered
the words of his neighbour who had
bought Smasher's sister.

"He's more like a bull mastiff than a
collie," he had said.

"You are, too," he said now. "And as for
ugly, well, I don't know so much about
that. Maybe I've just got used to the way
you look, with that wrinkly pushed-in
face of yours, but I wouldn't call you ugly.

True, you're not as handsome as some but all the same you've growed into a fine strong dog. You look – what's the word I want? – noble. Yes, that's it, noble."

On the Saturday that he was going to yard the bullocks, Farmer Buzzard said to Smasher, "You don't know it, my son, but you'll be spending this night in the stable."

What he did not know was that
Smasher would be spending that night in
the farmhouse.

Fate, in the shape of another dog, took a
hand in the matter.

Just as the farmer was about to set off
with Kay to take the bullocks down to the
field-barn, the phone rang.

Mrs Buzzard answered it.

"Yes?" she said. "Oh, no! Oh dear, oh
dear! Oh, yes. Of course. Yes. No. Yes. No.
Straight away."

"What was all that about, Martha?"
asked her husband.

"That was our Bertha," said Mrs
Buzzard.

Mrs Buzzard's unmarried sister Bertha
lived in the nearby town, alone save for
her dog, a much-spoiled Pekingese.

"That May-Wong of hers," went on Mrs
Buzzard, "tripped her up and she fell

down the stairs. Nothing broken, doctor
says, but she's ever so bruised and she
wants me to come for a few days and look
after her. You could manage, couldn't
you, Ken?"

"I dare say," replied Farmer Buzzard.

"You'll have Kay for company."

Not only Kay, thought the farmer.

"You don't mind, then?"

"Not pertickerly," said Farmer Buzzard.

That evening, when Mrs Buzzard had
gone to her sister's and the bullocks were
safely yarded down at the field-barn,
Farmer Buzzard sat comfortably in his
favourite chair, watching the telly. At his
feet lay his dogs.

Farmer Buzzard enjoyed television.
Recently he had treated himself to a
brand-new set, the latest model, with a
very big screen.

When it had arrived, Mrs Buzzard had
said, "You want to put a rug or summat
over that thing night times."

"Whatever for?" said Farmer Buzzard.

"Burglars," said Mrs Buzzard. "There's
been a lot of it about, breaking into
people's houses and taking their tellies
and video recorders and that. They look
through the window and see that great
thing, they'll have it."

"That's in town," said Farmer Buzzard.
"They don't come out here."

Now, at bedtime, he pointed the remote control at his pride and joy and switched it off.

Then he put the dogs out for a run.

Then he shut Kay up in the stable.

"I hopes your feelings won't be hurt, old girl," he said, "but I want Smasher to be on his own in the house for the night. If he's going to do anything naughty, it's better done while Martha's away."

Inside the house, he put an old blanket on the floor beside his chair and made Smasher lie down on it.

"Now you be a good boy," he said. "You're not a pup any more, you're a dog, so you behave yourself." And he climbed the stairs to bed.

This is the life, thought Smasher drowsily, at last I'm a house dog, and he fell happily asleep.

He slept so soundly that he did not hear stealthy footsteps outside the window in the middle of the night. Nor did he hear the slight scraping noise as the window was expertly forced. What woke him was in fact a stifled sneeze.

The burglar had shone his torch upon the television set and had just unplugged it, when he felt the sneeze coming on and hastily pressed a forefinger above his upper lip.

For a moment he stood stock still, listening in case the slight noise should have woken anyone upstairs. But then he in turn heard a slight noise.

Turning round, he shone his torch, and there, standing directly between him and the open window, was the largest, ugliest dog he had ever seen.

6. New Dog

Hullo, said Smasher to himself, who's this then? Must be a pal of the master's, come to stay, and, being a friendly dog, he advanced towards the man, tail wagging, ugly mouth agape in what was actually a smile but looked in the torchlight like an angry snarl.

"Good dog," whispered the burglar in a shaky voice, and Smasher, encouraged by this, leapt up and put his large paws on the man's chest.

The burglar was a small man, and he fell backwards under the weight of the dog, and began to shout "No! No! Get him off me! Help!"

Good game this, Smasher thought, and he began to bark loudly with excitement.

Woken by the hubbub, Farmer Buzzard

hurried downstairs, snatching his gun
from its cupboard on the way. He opened
the door of the room and switched on the
lights, to see Smasher standing on the
man's chest and giving his face a
thorough washing with a large slobbery
tongue, while the burglar still cried,
indistinctly now, for help.

Farmer Buzzard looked at the open
window and then at the unplugged
television set.

Martha was right, he thought.

He pointed to Smasher's blanket and said "Down!" and Smasher obeyed.

Then he waved his gun towards the prostrate burglar and said, "And you stay down too or my dog'll tear your throat out."

Then he rang the police.

"The master was ever so pleased with me, Mum," said Smasher to Kay when they met the next morning.

"What happened, dear?" asked Kay. "I heard you barking in the middle of the night, and then later on I heard a car drive up, and then voices. What was it?"

"I don't really know, Mum," said Smasher. "A man came and I thought he was a friend of the master's and I had a bit of a game with him. But then some other men came dressed in blue and wearing funny hats, and they took him away in a car with his hands sort of tied together."

"Handcuffs," said Kay. "Policemen! He must have been a burglar. He came to steal something, and you stopped him, dear!" And, just as her master had done, she said, warmly, "*What* a good boy!"

One evening a week later Mrs Buzzard returned. She found her husband sitting watching the telly, the remote control in his hand, the collie at his feet. In the next room there was, though she did not know it, another dog, lying still and silent as he had been told to do.

"Well, Ken," she said, kissing the top of his head. "You been all right?"

Farmer Buzzard nodded.

Conversation was not possible with him, Mrs Buzzard knew, while he was watching television, so she waited until

the programme had ended and then said,
"Everything been all right here?"

Farmer Buzzard switched off.

"You were right, Martha," he said.

"What about?"

"Burglars. We had one, the first night
you was away."

"Never!"

"Yes. After my telly, he was."

"I told you!" Mrs Buzzard said. "I said

you ought to cover it up night times. But
he never got it then?"

"No," said Farmer Buzzard.

"You caught him?"

"No. My dog caught him."

"Oh, Kay!" cried Mrs Buzzard. "*What* a
good dog!" And she bent to stroke the
collie.

"No, not Kay," said her husband. "My
new dog."

"New dog?"

"Yes. The very day you went to
Bertha's, it was. After what you said
about burglars, I thought to meself – what
we need is a proper house dog, a big
strong animal that will guard the place,
one that no burglar would face."

"So you went out and got one?"

"I went out," said Farmer Buzzard
truthfully, "and I got one. And by the
time I got downstairs that night, he'd

knocked the burglar down and he was standing on him. 'He'll tear your throat out,' I said to the man. We needn't worry about burglars any more."

"Well, I never!" said Mrs Buzzard. "Where is he then, this new dog?"

For answer Farmer Buzzard stood up and opened the connecting door and said "Come!" and in walked Smasher.

"Sit!" said the farmer, and he sat.

"Down!" said the farmer, and he lay down, tail gently wagging, a big grin on his wrinkly, pushed-in face.

"He won't tear my throat out, will he?" said Mrs Buzzard, a trifle nervously.

Farmer Buzzard laughed.

"Never!" he said. "He's a soft old thing, he is."

Like you, thought Mrs Buzzard, as she took a proper look at the dog.

"It's a funny thing," she said, "but I tell you who he reminds me of. I know I haven't got my proper spectacles on, but he puts me in mind of that puppy we got

rid of, you know, the one that did all that damage, that Smasher."

"That's what I call this dog, too," said Farmer Buzzard.

"You're right, he is a big strong dog," said Mrs Buzzard. "We'll be all right with him in the house. Though he's no beauty, mind. How would you describe him, what's the word?"

"Noble," said her husband.

Mrs Buzzard nodded.

"But doesn't he remind you of that ugly puppy too?" she asked, innocently.

"Not pertickerly," said Farmer Buzzard.

Also in Young Puffin

THE Hodgeheg

Dick King-Smith

Max is a hedgehog who becomes a hodgeheg, who becomes a hero!

The hedgehog family of Number 5A are a happy bunch, but they dream of reaching the Park. Unfortunately, a very busy road lies between them and their goal and no one has found a way to cross it in safety. No one, that is, until the determined young Max decides to solve the problem once and for all...

Also in Young Puffin

The Swoose

Dick King-Smith

"Are you feather-brained?" said the vole. "No, I'm Fitzherbert."

Fitzherbert is confused. With his oversized feet and snaky neck, he is shunned by the other goslings. Then his mother reveals that he is a rare breed of bird indeed – the offspring of her romantic liaison with a dashing white swan. With stars in his eyes, Fitzherbert sets off in search of his father and discovers fame beyond the farmyard in the household of the Queen of England herself!

'Other writers who put words into animals' mouths are outclassed'
– *The Times Educational Supplement*

'Judy Brown's enchanting black and white illustrations capture the spirit of both swoose and sovereign'
– *Independent on Sunday*

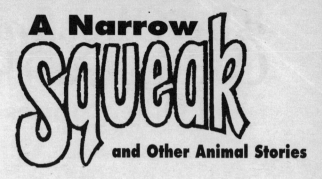

A Narrow Squeak

and Other Animal Stories

Dick King-Smith

**Be they soft and furry, sharp and prickly
or smooth and scaly, all the animals in
this collection are quite irresistible!**

A mouse is dicing with death in the larder,
while another is carried off in the jaws of a
fox. Then there's a bullied brontosaurus,
a wimpish woodlouse, a rebellious hedgehog
and a dog with an identity crisis.

'Other writers who put words into animals'
mouths are outclassed' – *The Times
Educational Supplement*

Also in Young Puffin

The Ghost *at* Codlin Castle

and Other Stories

Dick King-Smith

Have you ever wondered what it's like to carry your head under your arm? Or tried to guess what garden gnomes get up to after dark?

In this marvellously varied collection of stories, Dick King-Smith introduces some fascinating characters: a baby yeti, a bald hobgoblin and an extraordinary sausage-shaped alien among them.

Funny, mysterious, sinister, these gripping tales make ideal bedtime reading. With remarkable illustrations by Amanda Harvey, this is a book to stir the imagination.

Also in Young Puffin

GEORGE SPEAKS

Dick King-Smith

Laura's baby brother George was four weeks old when it happened.

George looks like an ordinary baby, with his round red face and squashy nose. But Laura soon discovers that he's absolutely *extraordinary*, and everyone's life is turned upside down from the day George speaks!

READ MORE IN PUFFIN

For children of all ages, Puffin represents quality and variety – the very best in publishing today around the world.

For complete information about books available from Puffin – and Penguin – and how to order them, contact us at the appropriate address below. Please note that for copyright reasons the selection of books varies from country to country.

On the worldwide web: www.puffin.co.uk

In the United Kingdom: Please write to *Dept. EP, Penguin Books Ltd, Bath Road, Harmondsworth, West Drayton, Middlesex UB7 ODA*

In the United States: Please write to *Consumer Sales, Penguin USA, P.O. Box 999, Dept. 17109, Bergenfield, New Jersey 07621-0120.* VISA and MasterCard holders call 1-800-253-6476 to order Penguin titles

In Canada: Please write to *Penguin Books Canada Ltd, 10 Alcorn Avenue, Suite 300, Toronto, Ontario M4V 3B2*

In Australia: Please write to *Penguin Books Australia Ltd, P.O. Box 257, Ringwood, Victoria 3134*

In New Zealand: Please write to *Penguin Books (NZ) Ltd, Private Bag 102902, North Shore Mail Centre, Auckland 10*

In India: Please write to *Penguin Books India Pvt Ltd, 706 Eros Apartments, 56 Nehru Place, New Delhi 110 019*

In the Netherlands: Please write to *Penguin Books Netherlands bv, Postbus 3507, NL-1001 AH Amsterdam*

In Germany: Please write to *Penguin Books Deutschland GmbH, Metzlerstrasse 26, 60594 Frankfurt am Main*

In Spain: Please write to *Penguin Books S. A., Bravo Murillo 19, 1° B, 28015 Madrid*

In Italy: Please write to *Penguin Italia s.r.l., Via Felice Casati 20, I-20124 Milano.*

In France: Please write to *Penguin France S. A., 17 rue Lejeune, F-31000 Toulouse*

In Japan: Please write to *Penguin Books Japan, Ishikiribashi Building, 2-5-4, Suido, Bunkyo-ku, Tokyo 112*

In South Africa: Please write to *Longman Penguin Southern Africa (Pty) Ltd, Private Bag X08, Bertsham 2013*